# Geronimo Stilton

# HEROMICE

## THE INVISIBLE THIEF

Scholastic Inc.

The publisher does not have any control over and does not assume any responsibility for author or third-party websites or their content.

Published by Scholastic Inc., 557 Broadway, New York, NY 10012. SCHOLASTIC and associated logos are trademarks and/or registered trademarks of Scholastic Inc.

*Stilton is the name of a famous English cheese. It is a registered trademark of the Stilton Cheese Makers' Association. For more information, go to www.stiltoncheese.com.*

This book is a work of fiction. Names, characters, places, and incidents are either the product of the author's imagination or are used fictitiously, and any resemblance to actual persons, living or dead, business establishments, events, or locales is entirely coincidental.

ISBN 978-0-545-92755-0

Text by Geronimo Stilton
Original title *Due supertopi contro il ladro invisibile*
Original design of the Heromice world by Giuseppe Facciotto and Flavio Ferron
Cover by Giuseppe Facciotto (design) and Daniele Verzini (color)
Illustrations by Luca Usai (pencils), Valeria Cairoli (inks), and Daniele Verzini (color)
Graphics by Chiara Cebraro and Francesca Sirianni

Special thanks to Kathryn Cristaldi
Translated by Andrea Schaffer
Interior design by Kevin Callahan / BNGO Books

10 9 8 7 6 5 4 3 2 1          15 16 17 18 19

Printed in the U.S.A                    40
First printing 2015

THEY'RE FAMOUSE . . .
THEY'RE FABUMOUSE . . .
AND THEY'RE HERE
TO SAVE THE DAY!
THEY'RE THE

# HEROMICE

AND THESE ARE THEIR
ADVENTURES!

When darkness falls over Muskrat City, the Sewer Rats slither into the alleys to cause chaos aboveground. But the citizens of Muskrat City know that there are mysterious figures watching over them, ready to fight evil at all costs.
They are strong, they are invincible, they are fearless — well, almost . . .
They are the Heromice!

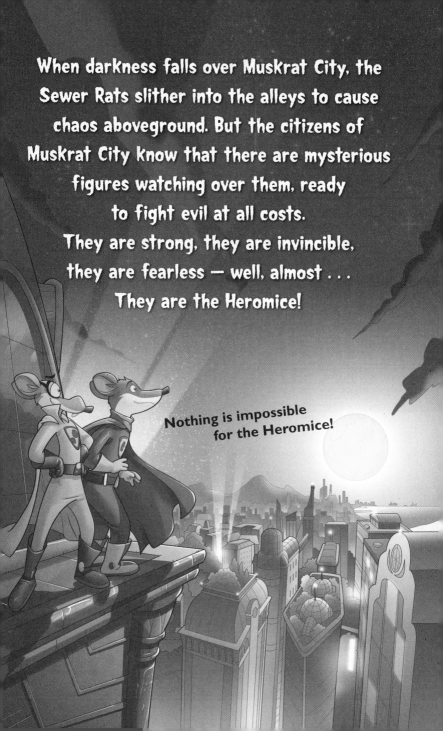

Nothing is impossible for the Heromice!

# MEET THE HEROMICE!

## GERONIMO SUPERSTILTON

The strongest hero in Muskrat City . . . but he still must learn how to control his powers!

## SWIFTPAWS

Geronimo Superstilton's partner in crimefighting; he can transform his supersuit into anything.

## LADY WONDERWHISKERS

A mysterious mouse with special powers; she always seems to be in the right place at the right time.

## TESS TECHNOPAWS

A cook and scientist who assists the Heromice with every mission.

## ELECTRON AND PROTON

Supersmart mouselets who help the Heromice; they create and operate sophisticated technological gadgets.

# ONY SLUDGE

The undisputed leader of the Sewer Rats; known for being tough and mean.

# RESA LUDGE

Tony's wife; makes the important decisions for their family.

# ENA SLUDGE

ony and Teresa's teenage ughter; has a real weakness for rat metal music.

# AND THE SEWER RATS!

# SLICKFUR

Sludge's right-hand mouse; the true (and only) brains behind the Sewer Rats.

# ONE, TWO, AND THREE

Bodyguards who act as Sludge's henchmice; they are big, buff, and brainless.

# So Long, Cheddar Chip!

It was a fabumouse sunny day in New Mouse City, the perfect day to **stretch** my paws in the park. Besides enjoying the great weather and getting some exercise, I couldn't wait to grab an ice cream from my favorite park vendor, The Cheesy Freeze. Have you been there? The Freeze makes the most whisker-licking-good treats!

But what a scatterbrain I am—I didn't introduce myself. My name is Stilton, *Geronimo Stilton*, and I am the editor in chief of *The Rodent's Gazette*, the most *famouse* newspaper on Mouse Island.

Anyway, where was I? Oh, yes, when I reached the park, I ordered my ice cream, but before I could take one nibble—**RRRING**! My cell phone rang.

Rats! I hoped whoever was calling would make it quick. My ice cream was already *melting*!

"Hello, hello, hello? Are you there, Geronimo?"

It was Hercule Poirat, my good friend and Heromouse partner.

"Hercule, is everything okay?" I asked.

"Far from it!" Hercule squeaked. "I need you in Muskrat City immediately! It's an emergency!"

"**EMERGENCY?** But . . . m-m-my ice cream —" I stammered.

Hercule interrupted me. "I'll explain everything when you get here, Geronimo! Just hurry up!"

I tried to protest, but all I heard was a **dial tone**.

What could I do? Hercule needed my help.

H-here goes . . .

Wiping away a tear, I stared longingly at my super delicious ice cream. "So long, cheddar chip!" I sighed. Then I looked for a place to transform into **SUPERSTILTON**!

I ducked behind the ice cream cart. This would be the **perfect** place! Then I pushed the secret button on my **Superpen**.

Immediately, a **green** ray of light enveloped me from my whiskers to my tail, transforming me into Superstilton!

5

Too bad I forgot two **tiny** details . . .

1) I had used the Superpen a little **too close** to the ice cream cart, and

2) I still had my *ice cream cone* in my paw.

So, right as I lifted up into the air, I became **tangled** in the cart awning. I tore the awning right off the cart, carrying it away with me!

Oh, why did I always feel like such a **superdunce** when it came to using my Superpen?!

# A Respectful Robbermouse

By the time I was able to get the awning off my snout, I could see Muskrat City below me. With the cloth **wrapped** around my supersuit, I landed in the garden of **Heromice Headquarters**.

"Super Swiss slices!" Swiftpaws cried when he saw me. "What is that, **SUPERSTILTON**?! A new supercape? A superdress?? A supertoga???"

I coughed, pretending I didn't notice I was wrapped up like a furry *supersausage*.

"Everything's under control," I muttered, freeing myself and changing the subject. "So, why don't you explain what's going on? Why did you call me? What's the **emergency**?"

"Hold up, **Superpartner**!" Swiftpaws squeaked. "I don't know anything!"

*Wait, what? Had I just given up a triple-decker* **Cheesy Freeze** *cone for nothing?*

Luckily, Commissioner Rex Ratford had just arrived.

"We have a very special case on our paws.

A case I'm hoping you *Heromice* can help solve," he said.

Right then, my hero watch activated, and **TESS TECHNOPAWS**, the supersmart scientist and cook at Heromice Headquarters, appeared on the screen.

"Welcome, Superstilton," she said to me. "Please come to the control room. I can explain everything."

A moment later, Swiftpaws, Commissioner Ratford, and I gathered together at the Heromice secret base.

Proton and **ELECTRON**, the youngest members of the group, were working in front of the supercomputer.

"Hi, Superstilton!" squeaked Proton.

Electron gave me a curious look. "How was your trip?" she asked, staring at my supersuit.

It was then that I realized I had STICKY ice cream and a squashed cone stuck to my supersuit. "Ahem, well, you see, the ice cream, I mean, the awning, I mean, the Superpen—" I tried to explain.

"We don't need the play-by-play," Swiftpaws said, cutting me short. "Now, can you tell us what **happened**, Commissioner?"

The head of police nodded. "I want you to take a look at the film from the security cameras of a few jewelers in the city. It seems they have been burgled by a very S P E C I A L thief called the Respectful Robbermouse."

"Why respectful?" I asked.

"It's the *nickname* they gave him on TV," explained Proton.

"The Respectful Robbermouse

always leaves a letter of apology at the scene of the crime," added Electron.

"Take a look at this," said Ratford, showing us a note *written* by paw.

Dear Commissioner,

So sorry to steal and run, but I really need these diamonds!

I hope you will forgive me. Please tell the owners of the jewelry store I will return the gems as soon as possible.

Sworn by an honorable rodent.

"Hmm . . . it is very polite," I said.

"It's very **fishy**, if you ask me!" snorted Ratford. "I've never met a thief who brings back the loot!"

"That's true," I agreed. "But I still don't understand why you called, Commissioner. Why did you say this is a **case** for the Heromice?"

At this, Ratford passed a flash drive to Proton, who inserted it into the **supercomputer**. Immediately, it showed the film from the security camera at **SQUEAKY BLINGS**, the most expensive and **elegant** jewelry store in Muskrat City.

It was after hours, and the store was closed.

There was no one in sight.

In the image, you could see a diamond sheltered by a **GLASS** dome.

"Watch carefully . . ." Ratford whispered.

The door of the store swung **open** **1**, as if it had been thrown open by a gust of wind.

# SWISH!

The alarm began to ring, and the glass dome lifted.

**CLICK!**

The diamond rose into the air and **floated** out the door of the jewelry store!

**WHOOSH!**

Holey cheese sticks!

Swiftpaws and I **GAWKED** at the computer screen.

"Now do you understand why I

**1.** The door suddenly opened . . .

**2.** The dome lifted . . .

**3.** The diamond floated out the door!

need you?" Commissioner Ratford asked, a **SUPERWORRIED** expression on his snout. "We are being plagued by an invisible thief!"

# THE STAR-STUDDED GEMSTONE

A shiver ran down my spine.

"But what if it's a **special effect**, Commissioner?" asked Electron.

"What if it's a practical joke?" added Proton.

"What if it's a gh-gh-ghost?!" I stammered, my whiskers **trembling** with fear.

"My **TECH MICE** have already checked everything, and they can't figure it out," the commissioner continued. "We need you, Heromice!"

**Twisted cat tails!** How were we supposed to stop an invisible thief?!

"We could watch all the jewelry stores

in the city by using a video link," Proton suggested. "That way when the thief strikes again —"

"There isn't time!" interrupted Commissioner Ratford. "Duchess Marilyn Mousekovia arrives today!"

"Who?" asked Swiftpaws.

The commissioner explained that Duchess Mousekovia is a rich and famous rodent who is friends with **PETE POWERPAWS**, the mayor of Muskrat City. There was going to be a fancy reception in her honor at Muskrat City's **GRAND HOTEL**.

"The duchess will be wearing the **Star-Studded Gemstone** tonight," the commissioner added. "It's a really enormouse, *priceless* diamond!"

"What an irresistible lure for the Invisible Thief!" Electron squeaked.

**"BLISTERING BLUE CHEESE!"** exclaimed Swiftpaws. "Let's shake a paw and get down to the Grand Hotel **ASAP**! We'll set a trap, so when the thief arrives, he won't know what hit him!"

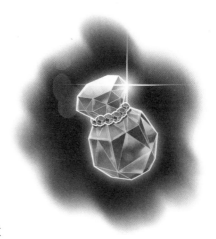

"Are you s-s-sure we need to go **right now**, Swiftpaws?" I stammered. *Oh, what I would give for a little downtime . . . a nice* **cheesy** *snack, a shower, or maybe a quick ratnap . . .*

Swiftpaws's squeak interrupted my thoughts. "Of course!" he insisted. "Remember, partner, criminals never stop! And neither do the Heromice!"

Before I could protest, Swiftpaws

**launched** into flight, dragging me with him! Our destination: Muskrat City's Grand Hotel!

A few minutes later, we arrived in the hotel ballroom. The place was bustling with activity. While the orchestra warmed up, the waiters scampered around, setting out a delicious-looking buffet.

I saw cheese sandwiches, bowls of cheesy pasta, and five fountains of creamy CHEESE FONDUE!

My stomach began to growl.

Gurgle, gurgle, gurgle!

I started drooling. That settled it. I needed a supersnack, and I needed it superfast! I edged closer to the fondue FOUNTAIN.

Unfortunately, before I could sneak one nibble, the others arrived. Proton began

mounting a SUPERSOPHISTICATED alarm in the hallway, while Swiftpaws, Commissioner Ratford, and I studied a **map** of the building.

"We need to check all the entrances! Every window and every door!" yelled Swiftpaws, running UP and **DOWN** the room.

Suddenly, an impeccably dressed rodent strode up to us.

"Gentlemice, can you *please* try not to be so loud and disruptive?" he implored, looking around nervously.

It was Snobby Le Fur, the manager of the Grand Hotel. "Remember that our guests are part of Muskrat City's high society," he added. "They expect only the best!"

Suddenly, a mouse swept into the room. She was wearing a gigantic diamond around her neck. It was the famouse **Star-Studded Gemstone**! So this was Duchess Marilyn Mousekovia!

The duchess **glared** at us. "Who are these rodents with the **Ratty** capes?" she asked Le Fur.

"Um, well, uh, they are part of the ***s-s-security team*** here at

Dear Duchess, it is an honor!

Hmm . . .

the Grand Hotel," stuttered Le Fur. "But I assure you that they won't be any bother to you or any of your guests."

"I hope not, **Le Fur**!" the duchess squeaked.

I shot a **look** at Swiftpaws.

"Don't worry, hero partner," he whispered. "I've got just the thing to spruce us up."

# SUPERHERO CLOWNS!

At six in the evening, the party began. All of Muskrat City's most important rodents gathered in the ballroom. Everyone was dressed in eLeGant formal wear.

Well, everyone except for Swiftpaws and me. We wore our usual supersuits along with enormouse bow ties!

Now, instead of looking like supermice, we looked like superclowns!

"Nice, huh?" said Swiftpaws, tweaking his bow tie proudly. Did I

Nice, huh?

mention my hero partner has no sense of fashion?

I glanced around the room. Not far from us I spotted the mayor chatting away with **Marilyn Mousekovia**. I inched closer, deciding to keep my eye on the duchess at all times. Who knew when the *Invisible Thief* might strike!

Suddenly, a voice broke into my thoughts. "Superstilton, how wonderful to see you!"

I turned, and felt my heart **THUMP** excitedly. It was *Priscilla Barr*, the most famouse lawyer in Muskrat City! She was with her father, Prosecutor Barr.

Priscilla was wearing a SPARKLING blue-green gown the same shade as her eyes. Besides being brilliant, Priscilla has a good **heart** and is a truly BEAUTIFUL mouse!

Immediately, I turned as **red** as my supercape.

"You're **wonderful**, er, I mean, I'm **wonderful**, uh, I mean, it's **wonderful** to see you, too," I babbled.

Oh, why am I such a mess around smart, attractive female mice?

I was telling Priscilla about our special **mission** when Swiftpaws ran over.

"There you are, hero partner!" Swiftpaws exclaimed. Then he noticed Priscilla. He grinned so **widely**

P-Priscilla . . .

I thought his jaw would **crack**. "May I have the honor of this dance, Miss Barr?" he asked, bowing before her.

"But, what about guarding the **Star-Studded Gemstone**?" I whispered to my partner.

"Relax!" Swiftpaws reassured me. "Everything is under control!"

I frowned. Forget about guarding the gemstone. My hero partner had just stolen the mouse of my **dreams** right out from under my whiskers!

**Rats!**

I decided to distract myself by **throwing** myself into my work.

I went off to look for the duchess. When I found her, I **BOWED** and asked her if she would like to dance.

"Um, do I know you?" she asked, staring

down her nose at me. Mayor Powerpaws
was standing close by.

"Dear Marilyn," he said. "This is Superstilton, one of the excellent defenders of Muskrat City!"

"Oh, yes, a *Heromouse*," the duchess snorted. "Now I recognize that terribly dreadful costume! Ugh! Don't you have anything else you can change into? Those boots are **hideous**! And the bow tie is ridiculous!"

I sighed. And to think I could have been dancing with the **sweet** and BEAUTIFUL Priscilla Barr!

I was just mumbling my apologies when suddenly I turned as pale as a slice of MOZZARELLA! The superdiamond that the duchess had been wearing around her neck had **DISAPPEARED**!

When I looked around, I couldn't believe my eyes! The Star-Studded Gemstone was **floating** right over the table of refreshments!

The *Invisible Thief* had struck again!

The duchess let out a tremendous scream.

"Nooooooooooo! My diamooooooooooooooooooond!!!"

Then she FAINTED, falling into my arms.

"Hey,    Invisible   Thief—stop!" yelled Commissioner Ratford. "Give   back   the diamond!"

"I'm sorry, but I can't!" responded a *nice* voice that came from the area near the floating diamond.

Swiftpaws and I looked at each other, dumbfounded.

# STOP, THIEF!

After the initial shock of seeing a *floating* diamond, Swiftpaws sprang into action.

"Get ready, Invisible Thief!" he squeaked, holding out his paws. "*Costume: Supernet Mode!*"

Immediately, my superpartner turned into an enormouse butterfly net! He raced after the flying gemstone. Unfortunately, he wasn't watching where he was going. A minute later — **BABAAAAM**!

Swiftpaws ran **SMACK** into one of the steaming fountains of fondue. The first fountain fell into the second, which fell into the third, which . . . well, you get the picture. It was one **Giant** cheesy mess!

Guests began slipping on the melted cheese that now **covered** the floor. The *Invisible Thief* took advantage of the chaos and fled with the diamond in his INVISIBLE paws!

"Oh no!" shrieked Ratford.

I noticed a trail of cheesy tracks that started from the table and went toward the staircase.

There wasn't a moment to lose. So, like a true **Heromouse**, I scampered after the thief, following his mysterious tracks.

I arrived on the top floor of the Grand Hotel and followed the tracks down a **long** hallway. But soon the tracks became LIGHTER, and then they disappeared altogether. I stopped and looked around, but I had no idea where the Invisible Thief had gone!

I continued to hear the sound of **FOOTSTEPS**, but I couldn't figure out where they were coming from!

"Soaking Swiss cheese milkshake!" I cried in exasperation. With those words, though, my cheesy superpowers activated.

# WHOOOSSSHHH!

A strong stream of **gloopy**, cheesy milkshake shot down the hallway. And thanks to the stream of liquid cheese, the Invisible Thief immediately became supervisible!

"Stop, thief!" I yelled.

But the agile rodent **zipped** through a door at the top of the stairs.

I followed him up the stairs until I found myself on the **rooftop** of the Grand Hotel. *Don't look down*, I thought. But I was already feeling very *dizzy*.

SUPERPOWER: **STREAM OF SWISS CHEESE MILKSHAKE** ACTIVATED WITH THE CRY: **SOAKING SWISS CHEESE MILKSHAKE!**

Argh!

Stop!

**Holey cheese sticks**, I'm afraid of heights!

"Surrender!" I shrieked.

Nothing happened. Then I thought I saw **something** peeking out from behind the chimney. I crept closer until . . .

"Superstilton, it's me!" a voice cried.

It was the smart, beautiful, and brave **Lady Wonderwhiskers**! Now I was really **dizzy**!

"**Lady Wonderwhiskers!**" I exclaimed. "What are you doing here?!"

Before I knew it, I was staring into Lady Wonderwhiskers's brilliant **blue** eyes as if in a trance. What strength! What **charm**! What a mouse!

"Is everything okay, Superstilton?" Lady Wonderwhiskers asked.

"No, I mean, yes, I mean—" I babbled.

I was interrupted by a very loud **SPLASSSSH**!

"It's the Invisible Thief!" exclaimed Lady Wonderwhiskers, pointing at the rooftop swimming pool.

A minute later, we saw a trail of puddles.

"What is he doing?" I asked, confused.

"It looks like he's heading for the **fire escape** ladder!" exclaimed Lady Wonderwhiskers. "Please do something, Superstilton!"

*Super Swiss slices!*

I could not disappoint the super-rodent of my heart!

So, even though my whiskers trembled with fear (Did I mention I'm terrified of heights?), I took a deep breath, crossed my whiskers for luck, and exclaimed, "Leave it to me, Lady Wonderwhiskers!"

Then I jumped with an amazing leap toward the fire escape and . . .

# Oooops!

I TRIPPED and tumbled off the edge of the roof. Luckily, my cape got caught on the metal railing! I was swinging in the air like a superklutz!

# YOU SAVED MY FUR!

Dangling high in the air from the roof of the Grand Hotel, headlines flashed before my eyes: *Super-rodent Meets Superend! Supersplat! Superfall for Superfool!*

"Hang on, Superstilton!" I heard Lady Wonderwhiskers call.

A second later, two **strong** paws grabbed me from behind and pulled me up to safety.

"Thank you, Lady Wonderwhiskers!" I exclaimed, still **trembling** with fear. "You saved my fur!"

But when I turned, I realized no one was there. Lady Wonderwhiskers was still on the other side of the roof!

"Wait, who saved me?!" I gasped.

"Me!" responded the Invisible Thief. "You see, I'm really not a **bad** mouse."

"But why are you **stealing** diamonds?" I demanded.

"I told you. I'm not stealing them!" the strange thief replied. "I'm borrowing them. I need them to help me **FIX** something. Then I'll return them. Rodent's honor!"

Thanks!

I got you!

I was still deciding what to do when suddenly I heard pawsteps racing down the fire escape.

Supersour cheddar chunks! The thief had escaped again!

"What do you think we should do, Lady Wonderwhiskers?" I squeaked, turning to face her. **CRUSTY CAT LITTER!** Now she had disappeared, too!

The only thing I could do was return to the floor below. But in the **BALLROOM**, the situation was out of control.

Duchess Marilyn Mousekovia was sitting on a bench, wailing,

"MY DIAMOOOOOND!
MYY DIAMOOOOOOOOOND!!
MYYYYY DIAMOOOOOOOOOOOOOOOOOOOOND!!!"

"Where have you been, Superstilton? I

YOU SAVED MY FUR!

can't solve this case by myself!" Swiftpaws yelled when he spotted me. "We've got to find that DIAMOND superfast!"

Before I could explain about the roof and the thief and the dangling in midair, Proton and ELECTRON arrived.

"Good news, Heromice!" Electron exclaimed. She was clutching a **strange contraption** in her paws. "We might have found a way to expose the Invisible Thief!"

"Let's meet back at **Heromice Headquarters**!" added Proton.

# WATCH YOUR TAILS!

Back at the base, Swiftpaws and I quickly washed our **sticky** supersuits so we didn't smell like **CHEESY FONDUE** and Swiss shakes. Then we dashed into the control room, where Proton and Electron had connected their **strange** contraption to the supercomputer.

Electron pointed to the screen. "Check out Tess Technopaws's latest invention, Heromice!" she exclaimed.

"It's an **invisible camera**!" added Proton.

The Heromice's official cook and scientist, Tess, arrived with a tray of **spicy** Gorgonzola **cream puffs**. "Oh, it's

nothing," she said modestly. "It's just a camera with a special sensor, a micro lens, and an inframouse ray—"

"I have no idea what that means," Swiftpaws interrupted. "But these snacks look delicious, Tess!"

"Swiftpaws is right!" I confirmed, DROOLING. "They look superamazing!"

Within seconds, Swiftpaws and I were chomping away like **starving** lab rats.

# CHomP! CHomP! CHomP!

"What that means is that this camera can photograph invisible images," Electron explained, shooting us a disapproving **look**.

A minute later, a picture appeared on the screen. It was the *Invisible Thief*!

"But that's *Jack Griffmouse*, one

of the most famouse inventors in Muskrat City!" squeaked Tess.

"That's odd. I haven't seen him in a while," commented Tess.

File No. 723576
Jack Griffmouse

Who: inventor and professor of applied cybernetics at the University of Muskrat City

Where he lives: in an old house on the outskirts of Muskrat City

Strength: He's supercreative.

Weakness: He's supermessy.

"You haven't **SEEN** him because he's been invisible!" Swiftpaws snickered as he **stuffed** another cheese puff into his mouth.

I reached for another one myself. After all, I didn't want my hero partner eating alone.

"Something's fishy here," continued Tess. "Griffmouse is an honest rodent. I don't know why he would be stealing *diamonds*."

"Well, there's only one way to find out," concluded Swiftpaws. "Let's go on a surveillance mission at his house!"

I tried not to choke. Go to the *Invisible Thief's* house?

# Oh, what a fright

Before I could stop him, Swiftpaws called

Commissioner Ratford to explain our plan to visit the *Invisible Thief*.

"Great idea!" Ratford said. "Good luck, **HEROMICE**! And please, watch your tails!"

# Swish . . . Swish . . . Swish!

Jack Griffmouse's house was on the other side of Muskrat City. The plan was to fly there, but I was having a little trouble LIFTING off. Well, okay, I was having a LOT of trouble! So Swiftpaws shouted: "Costume: Superflying Scooter Mode!"

I hopped on board, and before long, we landed in front of an old crumbling house that was surrounded by overgrown trees and bushes.

My whiskers started to tremble with fear. What a scary place!

"Are you sure th-this is a g-good idea?" I stammered.

"**Shhhhhhhh!** What are you trying to do, get caught, hero partner? Why don't you just ring the doorbell?" Swiftpaws snorted.

He snuck up to the back porch. We were in luck (if you call sneaking into a **S P O O K Y** house at night lucky!) — the back door was open.

But just as we were about to enter, we heard a sound . . .

## Swish . . . Swish . . . Swish!

Something was moving in the bushes behind us!

"This time he's not getting away!" whispered Swiftpaws. "*Costume: Supernet Mode!*"

Instantly, Swiftpaws's costume transformed into an enormouse butterfly net. He launched it into the bushes.

**Swish! Bonk! Thump!**

"Super Swiss slices! I've GOT you!" my superpartner cried.

"Oof! Stop!" exclaimed an unmistakable female voice.

## GREAT BALLS OF MOZZARELLA!

It was Lady Wonderwhiskers!

"Rats!" said Swiftpaws. He seemed superdisappointed it wasn't the thief. "Sorry about that, Lady Wonderwhiskers. But what are you doing here?"

Look!

"Did you think I would let you do this alone?" asked the super-rodent, her blue eyes TWINKLING.

Ah, Lady Wonderwhiskers. She was so brilliant and beautiful. A mouse could get lost staring into those sparkling blue eyes. Funny, they reminded me of another lady rodent I admired . . .

I was still thinking about those eyes when Lady Wonderwhiskers held up a small gadget that emitted a **blue flashing light**.

"What's that?" Swiftpaws asked.

"A position indicator," the super-rodent explained. "Tess Technopaws gave it to me. You attach it to the object you're trying to follow and it transmits a signal to our **communicator** watches," she explained. "This way we can find anyone, no matter where they go!"

"Well, what are we waiting for?" squeaked Swiftpaws. "Let's go!"

# A SUPERSECRET!

Soon we were exploring Professor Griffmouse's house. There were rooms filled snout to tail with what looked like **scientific** books and MATH manuals. But we didn't see any diamonds.

"RATS!" whined Swiftpaws.

Then I checked the library.

Just then I noticed a small **green book** tucked into one corner of the shelf.

Curious, I picked it up. - - - - - - - - ->

**Slaaaaaaammmmmm!**

Suddenly, the wall of books began moving. Before I could **SQUEAK**, everything went **D A R K**. And I mean, super, **S U P E R D A R K**. I couldn't see my own paw in front of my whiskers!

"**HELP!**" I shrieked. "What happened?!"

"Looks like this library has a supersecret!" exclaimed Swiftpaws from the other side of the wall.

"Good job, Superstilton!" added Lady Wonderwhiskers. "You found a secret passage! Now all you have to do is turn the library around so we can come, too!"

A chill ran down my fur. "Turn the library?" I croaked. "But I don't know how!"

I tried not to SOB uncontrollably.

"Okay, concentrate, hero partner!" Swiftpaws said encouragingly. "Do you remember what you did before the wall turned?"

I blinked. "Well, um, I picked up a little GREEN book and . . ."

"Do you remember which book?" Lady Wonderwhiskers asked.

"Remember?" I squeaked. "How could I forget? I love books! I love biographies! I love mysteries! I love—"

"We get it, Superstilton! You're a bookrat!"

Swiftpaws interrupted. "Now, what's the title?"

But before I could reply . . .

*SLAAAAAAMMMMMM!*

The shelves turned again.

"Let's go!" squeaked Lady Wonderwhiskers, pointing a flashlight down a dark hallway.

**Heromice in action!**

We made our way down the **dark** corridor until we reached a large room filled with electronic equipment.

"Great galaxies! It's somebody's *secret laboratory*!" I gasped.

At one end of the room, a giant glass cylinder was clicking and humming away.

"Not **SOMEBODY'S** laboratory, Superpartner, it's the Invisible Thief's!" Swiftpaws announced.

"But how do you know?" I asked.

"Use your **SUPERVISION**, Superstilton!" Swiftpaws said, pointing at the cylinder.

I squinted. Then I *rubbed* my eyes. But I still didn't see a thing.

"Don't you see that screwdriver *floating*

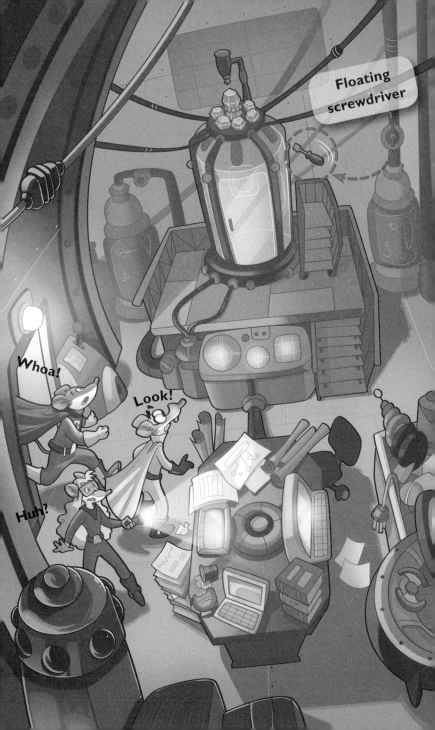

in the air around that machine?" whispered Lady Wonderwhiskers. "I'd bet our very own Invisible Thief is holding it!"

As we watched, the screwdriver began moving around a plate of diamonds. The **Star-Studded Gemstone** sparkled in the center!

My heart hammered.

"Wh-wh-what is he d-d-d-oing?" I stammered.

"Who knows?" replied Swiftpaws. "There's only one way to find out!"

With a squeak, he sprang into the center of the room.

*"Heromice in action!"*

he yelled.

# THE INVISIBILITY MACHINE

The screwdriver fell to the ground. "Oh no! Not you again!" We heard Griffmouse exclaim.

Then his pawsteps skittered across the laboratory floor. Super Swiss slices! The Invisible Thief was escaping . . . again!

"Hey, Griffmouse—stop!" shouted Lady Wonderwhiskers. "Tell us what's going on!"

"Right!" I added. "Maybe we can help you!"

The Invisible Thief's steps stopped suddenly. "Help me?" he asked.

"Well, uh, yes, you said you needed to fix something," I reminded him.

The steps came closer.

"Yes, exactly!" Griffmouse responded. "I need to repair my invention, the **Invisibility Machine**!"

I looked at the strange device at the back of the laboratory. *So that's what Griffmouse used to* transform *himself into the Invisible Thief!*

"One of the *SUPERLENSES* is broken, and I need to find a way to fix it quickly!" he continued.

Swiftpaws scratched his head. "But what do the *diamonds* have to do with it?" he asked.

I nodded. I must admit this supercase was getting superconfusing!

"I needed a lens similar to the one that broke," said Griffmouse. "That's why I needed the *purest* of diamonds. So

I had to borrow them from the jewelry stores. But I promise I'll return them! I just need to use the machine one last time."

We heard Griffmouse race back to his machine. Then we heard lots of clanging and banging. "I want to return to normal," he continued. "It's no fun being an invisible rodent. It's very lonely. No one says hi. No one smiles at me. No one wants to go to dinner or play baseball or go to the movies."

My friends and I didn't know what to say. Being an invisible rodent sounded awful.

Just at that moment . . .

# VROOOMMM!

"What is that noise?" I asked.

**VROOOOOOMMMM!**

The sound grew louder and louder!

Suddenly, a **WALL** of the laboratory crumbled into a cloud of **dust** and rubble, and the Sewer Rats' Sludgemobile zoomed

into the laboratory!

A second later, the evil Tony Sludge's bodyguards, **ONE**, **TWO**, and **Three**, quickly came running through the door.

The Sludgemobile!

Oh no!

Gulp!

Oh, whoops! I forgot to explain who the **CRUEL**, **revolting**, and always **stinky** Tony Sludge is: He's the leader of the truly terrible Sewer Rats!

# DON'T MAKE ME LAUGH!

**Crumbling cheese crackers!**
What were the Sewer Rats doing in
Griffmouse's secret laboratory?!

"The Invisibility Machine will be mine!"
Tony Sludge sneered. "And then Muskrat
City will be **mine, mine, mine**!"

"Not so fast, **SEWER
SLIME**!" Swiftpaws
challenged him.
"First you'll
have to get
past the
Heromice!"

"Don't
make me

*The Machine will be mine!*

laugh!" Tony scoffed. "Oh, and speaking of laughter, say hello to someone who will really get your giggles going, Superfools!"

Tony's right-hand mouse, SLICKFUR, emerged from the Sludgemobile. He wore a gas mask and a strange tank connected to a tube on his back.

Within minutes, a cloud of pink gas began seeping from the tank.

"You can't scare us with your colored gas . . ." my hero partner began. But before he could continue, he dissolved into a fit of giggles!

"Hee-hee! Hee-hee! Hee-hee!"

"Swiftpaws! Get a hold of yourself . . ." I began, until I started cracking up, too! "Ha, ha, ha! Ha, ha, ha! Ha, ha, ha!"

"Check it out, silly Superpests!" Slickfur

announced. "It's my latest, greatest invention: side-splitting, pink, paralyzing giggle gas!"

"**Hee-hee! Hee-hee! Ha, ha, ha!** Ho, ho, ho!" lovely Lady Wonderwhiskers laughed.

Here's my latest invention!

Oh no!

She had been struck by the giggle gas as well!

My hero partners and I couldn't stop rolling on

73

the ground. The incredible giggle gas was giving us full-blown **laugh** attacks!

One, Two, and Three caught us without difficulty, tied us together, and hung us from the ceiling like three **supercheese** sausages!

Then they grabbed the **Invisibility Machine** and secured it to the roof of the Sludgemobile.

"Good-bye, Superpests!" Tony called as

he climbed into the Sludgemobile and disappeared down the sewer.

VRRRRRROOMM!

Good-bye, superpests!

Ho, ho, ho!

HEE HEE HO HA

# DON'T MOVE, SUPERSTILTON!

The effects of the *giggle gas* eventually wore off. But we were still tied up.

"**Moldy mozzarella muffins!**" Swiftpaws exclaimed. "We must *FREE* ourselves!"

"But how?" I cried. "I can't **MOVE**!"

Then a ladder moved underneath us. A pair of scissors floated into the air.

"Don't move, **Superstilton**!"

It was the *Invisible Thief*!

I watched the **sharp** pointy scissors coming toward me and cringed. I'm too fond of my fur!

A second later . . .

CLUNK! CLUNK! CLUNK! CLUNK!

I found myself lying on the ground.

In the meantime, Griffmouse also freed my supercolleagues.

"But where did you go, Griffmouse?" Lady Wonderwhiskers asked him.

"I was here the whole time," the professor explained. "I just didn't make a sound.

Being invisible has more than a few advantages."

Yes, if you were invisible, you could do all kinds of things — supergood things and **superbad** things!

"How did the Sewer Rats know about the Invisibility Machine?" I asked Griffmouse.

Griffmouse let out a deep, **long** sigh. "It's time to tell you everything from the beginning," he confessed.

"After years of failed attempts, last week I finally got my invention to work," the professor explained. "I was thrilled! But then I found out the Sewer Rats had been spying on me. Tony and SLICKFUR showed up at my house. They wanted to steal my invention!

"To escape from the Sewer Rats, I was forced to use the ray of invisibility on myself. Unfortunately, the Sewer Rats tried to block the machine and one of the lenses broke into

**SMITHEREENS**!"

"Now I understand," I said.

"The Sewer Rats escaped. They couldn't catch me, and the machine was out of service."

"So that's how you became the *Invisible Thief*!" exclaimed Lady Wonderwhiskers.

"Yes," Griffmouse continued sadly. "I tried everything I could think of to **replace** the broken lens and repair my

invention. I know it was wrong to steal the diamonds. But I didn't know what else to do!"

I have to admit, I felt bad for Griffmouse. Being invisible might sound fun at first, but I wouldn't want to be invisible **forever**, either. I'm too fond of my fur!

"It's okay," I told the professor. But when I tried to pat his shoulder reassuringly, I accidentally **smacked** him in the snout!

"Sorry about that," I apologized. "But don't worry. We'll help you!"

And so with SWIFTPAWS and Lady Wonderwhiskers by my side, we shouted:

## "HEROMICE TO THE RESCUE!"

# BEEP! BEEP! BEEP!

We took off into the tunnel carved by the Sludgemobile.

"**BLECH**, what a stench!" I said, plugging my nose.

"We are in the 𝕤𝕖𝕨𝕖𝕣𝕤 of Muskrat City!" exclaimed Swiftpaws. "What did you expect it to smell like, hero partner? **Cheddar Dreams Spritz & Spray?!**"

"Good one!" chuckled a voice behind me.

Blech!

I **whirled** around, but no one was there!

Rotten cheese rinds! Was the **stench** making me lose my mind? Or was there a ghost on our tails?

"D-d-don't hurt us," I **stammered**. "We come in p-p-peace."

"Don't be a superfool, Superstilton!" Swiftpaws scoffed. "It's Griffmouse!"

"Are you sure you want to come along, Professor?" asked Lady Wonderwhiskers. "It could be **DANGEROUS**."

"Don't worry," he squeaked with a laugh. "You won't even know I'm here."

Suddenly, Lady Wonderwhiskers's wrist communicator began pulsating.

Beep . . . Beep . . . Beep . . .

The amazing super-rodent had managed to attach the position signaler to the

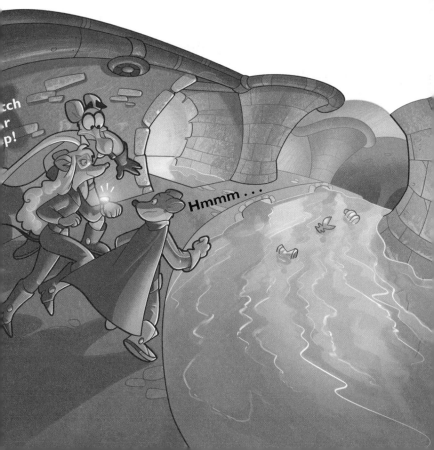

Sludgemobile! Now all we had to do was follow the signal!

Ah, Lady Wonderwhiskers! As we ran, I glanced at the super-rodent's bright sparkling eyes. She was so smart and beautiful and strangely familiar . . .

I was still thinking about Lady Wonderwhiskers when her wrist communicator began FLASHING at an alarming rate.

BEEP, BEEP, BEEP, BEEP, BEEP!

When I looked up, Tony, his henchmen, and the Sludgemobile were assembled in the tunnel in front of us.

"Oh no, they're going to turn on the Invisibility Machine!" whispered Griffmouse.

As we crept closer, we heard Slickfur say, "Duh, but, boss, why are we testing out the machine here? I thought we were bringing it back with us."

"Duh, I thought the same thing," agreed One.

"Me, too," added Two.

"Me, too," muttered Three. "I mean, me three, I mean, whatever they said."

Tony looked like he was ready to explode. He began to scream, waving his paws in the air like a crazed rat. "First of all, you shouldn't THINK! I'm the brains of this operation, and I do all the thinking around here! Got it?! I'm the boss, the big cheese, the head rodent!" Tony shrieked. "Anyway, I have a very good reason for testing the machine here. Her name is Mrs. Sludge. That's right. If my wife, Teresa, sees those diamonds, she'll rip that machine apart in a flash to get her paws on the Star-Studded Gemstone. Yep, Teresa sure loves her jewelry . . ."

While Tony *rambled* on and on, we crept closer and closer to the Sewer Rats. Finally, Lady Wonderwhiskers burst from the **shadows**.

"Give up, Sewer Slime!" she yelled.

The Sewer Rats' jaws dropped open in shock as the athletic super-rodent of my **heart** leaped forward. What a mouse!

# An Invisible Heromouse

Tony looked even angrier than before. "Now I'm really annoyed by you **Heromice**!" he squeaked in disgust. "Sewer Rats, give these *supergoons* the lesson they deserve!"

A second later, One *hurled* himself at Swiftpaws, but the Heromouse was one pawstep ahead of him.

I'm going to bowl you over!

"Costume: Bowling Ball Mode!" he yelled.

Instantly, Swiftpaws transformed into a giant YELLOW bowling ball. Then he rolled right into One and Two . . .

# Boiiiiiiiiinnnng!

. . . and sent them flying!

Meanwhile, Three had attacked Lady Wonderwhiskers. Unfortunately for him, he hadn't considered her INCREDIBLE martial arts skills!

BONK! SLAM! SMACK! POW! POP!

*Cosmic cheddar chunks!* Is there nothing the super-rodent of my dreams cannot do?

And so, in a matter of minutes, all three of Tony's bodyguards were laid out on the ground like pins in a bowling alley. STRIKE!

"Well, don't just lie there!" their boss yelled. "Get up, Rats! Capture those superpains! Do it now!"

Suddenly, I looked up to find Tony Sludge TOWERING over me. *Gulp!* He

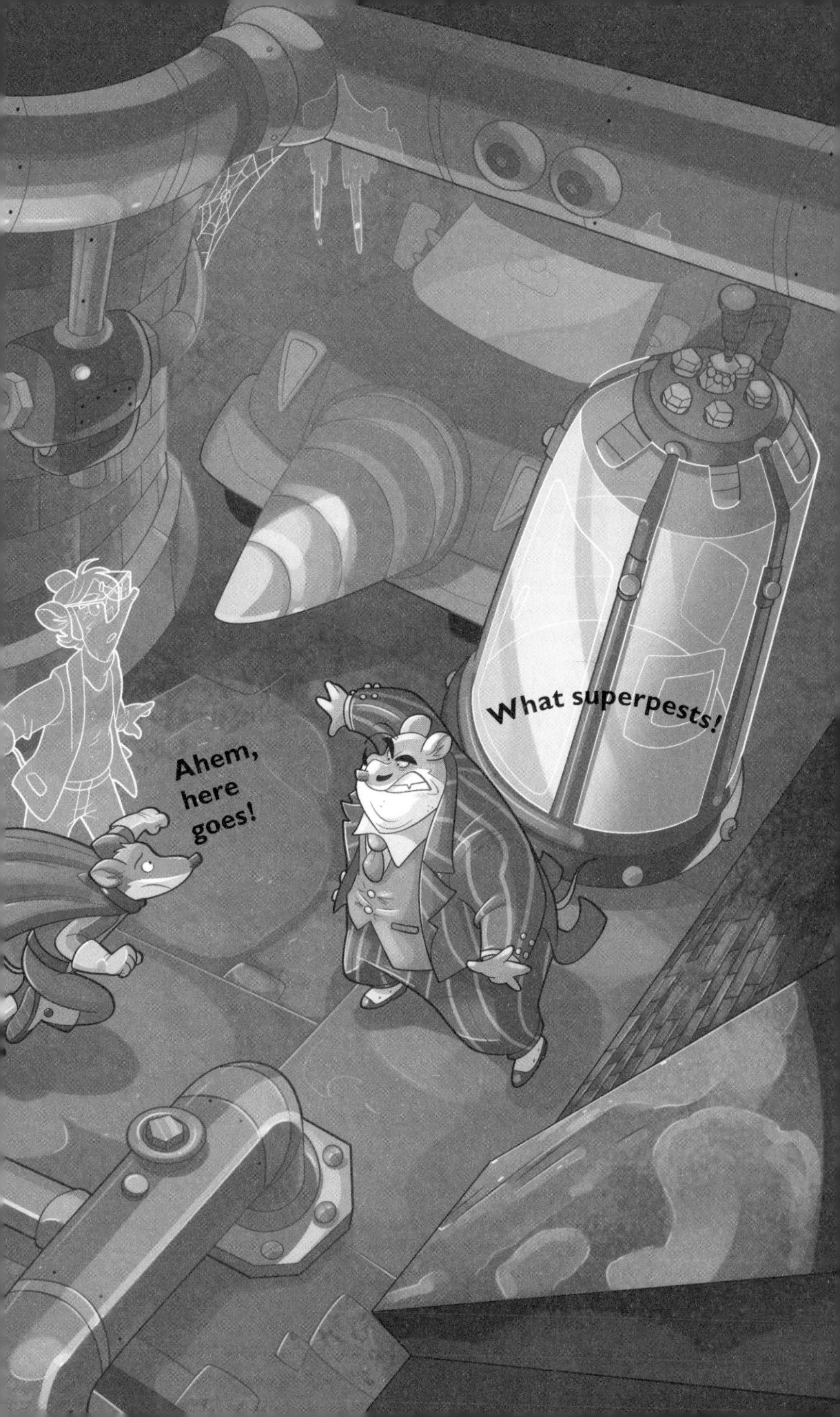
What superpests!
Ahem, here goes!

looked like he wanted to break every bone in my body!

But before I could turn tail and run (I told you, I'm not cut out to be a Heromouse!), an *invisible* paw grabbed me.

"I've got a great idea, Superstilton!" Griffmouse whispered in my ear. "While your hero partners distract the **Sewer Rats**, we'll turn on the Invisibility Machine. I'll make myself visible again and grab the **DIAMONDS**. Then I'll **destroy** my invention once and for all!"

Great Gouda! *Griffmouse's plan might actually work!*

So, while my friends tried to keep the Sewer Rats busy, Griffmouse and I quietly **scampered** up to the Invisibility Machine. Griffmouse jumped in and . . .

**BZZZZZTTTTT!**

Blue **LIGHTS** flashed, and slowly, a rodent figure appeared inside the machine.

*Finally!*

He had short **dark** hair and wore a white lab coat.

"**I did it!**" cheered Griffmouse, a wide grin on his snout.

But before we could celebrate our

success, Tony **SPOTTED** us.

"Stop them!" he ordered.

One dashed toward me, so I took a **superleap** 1.

Unfortunately when I hit the ground, I **tripped** over my cape 2 and bounced like a superball, coming to a stop when I hit my head. **BONK!** 3

Oof!

Superleap . . .

1

*Who am I? Where am I? What happened?!*

As I brushed myself off, I heard my superpartners squeaking at me.

"GET OUT OF THERE, SUPERSTILTON!" yelled Griffmouse.

"MOVE it!" shrieked Swiftpaws.

"*RUN!*" cried Lady Wonderwhiskers.

Huh? What were they talking about?

# BZZZZZTTTTT!

**FRYING FURBALLS!** By the time I realized I was inside the Invisibility Machine, it was too late!

A *flashing* light hit me!

I looked at my paws . . .

. . . they had become TRANSPARENT.

I looked at my tail . . .

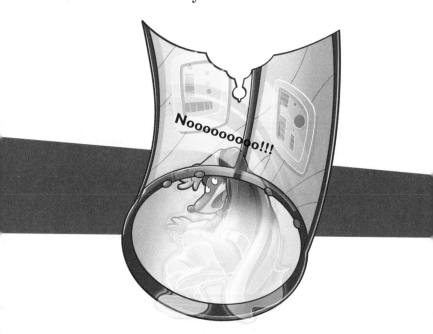

Nooooooooo!!!

. . . it wasn't there ANYMORE!

I looked at the tips of my whiskers and watched as they . . .

. . . disappeared!

Great galaxies! I had become an **invisible Heromouse**!

"Boss, look at that!" Slickfur said gleefully. "The machine works *perfectly*!"

In the meantime, Tony's evil assistant was putting on the gas mask and pointing the tube of side-splitting, pink, paralyzing giggle gas at Griffmouse and the other Heromice!

Ham and holey Swiss! We were in trouble again!

# BIG BOUNCING
# CHEESE BALLS!

"Put the Invisibility Machine on the Sludgemobile!" Tony instructed his henchmen.

As One, Two, and Three lifted the machine, Slickfur turned to my hero partners. "Prepare yourselves, Superfools!" he squeaked. "You're about to be paralyzed . . . with **LAUGHTER**!" the evil rodent snickered. "**Hee-hee-hee!** I crack myself up!"

Slickfur was still chuckling to himself when Swiftpaws whispered. "It's up to you, Superstilton!"

I **froze**. How could I *SAVE THE DAY*?!

I had to think of **SOMETHING**. Everyone was counting on **me**, Geronimo Stilton. No, scratch that. They were counting on **me**, Geronimo Superstilton!

Suddenly, I had an idea. I crept up to Slickfur without making a sound. As Griffmouse said, being **invisible** had its advantages!

Then, right before the slimy Sewer Rat turned on the giggle gas, I had an idea.

"Swiftpaws, ACTIVATE FAN MODE!" I yelled to my hero partner.

As Slickfur sprayed the giggle gas at Swiftpaws, my hero partner transformed into an extralarge fan! With a huge blast of air, the gas shot back at Slickfur!

At the same time, I leaped at Slickfur, YANKING off his gas mask.

So in a matter of seconds, the evil Sewer Rat . . .

1) got blasted with the side-splitting, pink, paralyzing giggle gas and

2) began *rolling* on the ground and laughing like a crazed fan at the Bent Whiskers Comedy Cellar!

"HA, HA, HA! HA, HA, HA! HA, HA, HA! HA, HA, HA! HA, HA, HA! HA, HA, HA!"

"Good work, Superstilton!" Swiftpaws congratulated me.

Before we could celebrate, One, Two, and Three finished tying the **Invisibility Machine** on to the roof of the Sludgemobile. They picked up the giggling Slickfur and shoved him into the front of the car.

"Sewer Rats escaping!" yelled Lady Wonderwhiskers.

Tony climbed behind the wheel of the Sludgemobile and began **revving** the motor.

## VRRROOOMMM! VRRROOOMMM!

"So long, Supersaps!" Tony snorted with an evil sneer. "Thanks for testing out the **Invisibility Machine** for us!"

Oh no! This couldn't be happening!

"**Big bouncing cheese balls!**
We've got to stop them!" I yelled at the top
of my lungs.

And suddenly, a hailstorm of cheese balls
began to rain down!

BOING!  BOING!
BOING!  BOING!

The balls hit the Sludgemobile and
began **bouncing** all over the place. My

Wow!

Good hit!

superpowers had **saved** the day!

The car went into a **skid** and crashed.

SUPERPOWER:
**BOUNCING BALLS OF CHEESE** ACTIVATED WITH THE CRY: **BIG BOUNCING CHEESE BALLS!**

Ow, ow

CRAAAAASSSSH!!!

"That was incredible, Superstilton! You're awesome!" squeaked Lady Wonderwhiskers, admiringly.

"It was nothing," I said, turning as **RED** as a tomato. Luckily, I was still invisible, so the rodent of my dreams couldn't tell.

Unluckily, in the crash, the **Invisibility Machine** had flipped off the Sludgemobile and smashed onto the ground.

"**Putrid provolone!**" I sobbed. "The **Invisibility Machine** is ruined! Now I'll be invisible forever!"

I can fix it.

Griffmouse checked out the machine. "Don't worry," he assured me. "I can **FIX** it. I just need to get it back to my lab."

"That's the **GOOD NEWS**," Swiftpaws said. "Now for the **bad news**: The Sewer Rats are gone!" He pointed to the smashed-up Sludgemobile with the doors hanging wide open. There wasn't a Sewer Rat in sight!

"They *escaped* again!" cried Lady Wonderwhiskers.

"Well, at least we got the Invisibility Machine back, right?!" I said.

My superpartners agreed finding the machine was superimportant. But there was still one problem. The machine was so **HEAVY**! How would we be able to transport it back to the lab?

"I've got it!" exclaimed Swiftpaws. **"COSTUME: TRACTOR MODE!"**

Within seconds, Swiftpaws transformed himself into a large YELLOW tractor! We loaded up and took off!

# DESTROY THE MACHINE!

When we got back to the lab, the professor began working on the Invisibility Machine. I held my breath. Would he be able to fix it? I mean, my supersuit was pretty goofy-looking, but I still missed **SEEING** myself in it!

In the end, the professor got everything up and running. I stepped under the **blue** light and . . . **Bzzzzt!** I was visible again!

Then Griffmouse unscrewed the lens of *diamonds* and gave them to Lady Wonderwhiskers to hold for safekeeping.

Now the only thing left to do was **destroy** the machine. "It can't fall into the wrong paws again," said Griffmouse.

Swiftpaws handed me a mallet. "**Destroy** the machine!" he instructed.

"Me? Why me?" I muttered. "I can't do—"

"Of course, you can do it, Superstilton!" interrupted Lady Wonderwhiskers. "**You're a Heromouse!**"

I gulped, clutching the heavy mallet. "**Fuming fondue fountain!**" I squeaked. "I'm not cut out to be a Heromouse!"

Right then my awesome cheesy superpowers activated and . . .

*Splaaasshhh!*

A fountain of **melted** cheese hit the Invisibility Machine, causing it to short circuit. After a lot of **sparks** and **SPUTTERS**, it died.

"Now it's time to turn myself in," said Griffmouse.

When we arrived at the police station,

SUPERPOWER:
**CHEESY FONDUE FOUNTAIN**
ACTIVATED WITH THE CRY:
**FUMING FONDUE FOUNTAIN!**

Wow!

Oooh!

we filled in *Commissioner Ratford*. We told him how the professor had helped to foil the Sewer Rats' evil plans and how he had insisted on destroying the Invisibility Machine.

"Uh ..." the commissioner replied. "This case is a little unusual. First we must give back those diamonds. Then I'll figure out what to do about Professor Griffmouse."

So, accompanied by two agents, the Ex-Invisible Thief returned to the jewelry stores where he had stolen the diamonds and gave everything back.

In the end, the commissioner ordered the professor to pay a big **fine**. He also had to return the **Star-Studded Gemstone** to Duchess Mousekovia.

"Please accept my deepest apologies, Duchess," Griffmouse said with a bow. "I'm so sorry I had to steal from such a **charming** and beautiful rodent."

"Oh, Professor," beamed the duchess. "How could I not forgive such a fascinating gentlemouse like you?"

**Great balls of Feta!** Griffmouse had been a hit with Duchess Mousekovia!

As for me, it was time to return home. So I said good-bye to my friends and, after a few tries (okay, maybe six or seven!), I flew off toward New Mouse City . . .

**WHOOOOOOOSH!**

I was heading for the park I had departed

I'm so sorry!

Oh, Professor . . .

from. But instead of landing behind **THe CHeeSy FReeze** ice-cream stand, I crashed into the middle of a **THORNY** blackberry bush.

## CRASH!

The thorns stuck in my fur. **OUCH!** And, now that I was no longer in my supercostume, the blackberries had left ugly *blue stains* all over my favorite suit!

**cheese niblets!** I was a walking fashion disaster!

I slunk home, keeping my head down. But I still heard rodents giggling as I passed by. *Oh, what I wouldn't give to be* invisible! But then I remembered all the trouble being *invisible* had caused the professor. Maybe that was one superpower the Heromice could do without!

Anyway, I didn't need to be invisible to be a Heromouse. If there was one thing I had learned, it was this: Nothing is impossible for the **HEROMICE**!

See you on my next adventure!

# Be sure to read all my fabumouse adventures!

st Treasure of the Emerald Eye

#2 The Curse of the Cheese Pyramid

#3 Cat and Mouse in a Haunted House

#4 I'm Too Fond of My Fur!

#5 Four Mice Deep in the Jungle

Paws Off, eddarface!

#7 Red Pizzas for a Blue Count

#8 Attack of the Bandit Cats

#9 A Fabumouse Vacation for Geronimo

#10 All Because of a Cup of Coffee

t's Halloween, Fraidy Mouse!

#12 Merry Christmas, Geronimo!

#13 The Phantom of the Subway

#14 The Temple of the Ruby of Fire

#15 The Mona Mousa Code

Cheese-Colored Camper

#17 Watch Your Whiskers, Stilton!

#18 Shipwreck on the Pirate Islands

#19 My Name Is Stilton, Geronimo Stilton

#20 Surf's Up, Geronimo!

**#21 The Wild, Wild West**

**#22 The Secret of Cacklefur Castle**

**A Christmas Tale**

**#23 Valentine's Day Disaster**

**#24 Field Trip Niagara Fal**

**#25 The Search for Sunken Treasure**

**#26 The Mummy with No Name**

**#27 The Christmas Toy Factory**

**#28 Wedding Crasher**

**#29 Down and Down Under**

**#30 The Mouse Island Marathon**

**#31 The Mysterious Cheese Thief**

**Christmas Catastrophe**

**#32 Valley of the Giant Skeletons**

**#33 Geronimo o Gold Medal My**

**#34 Geronimo Stilton, Secret Agent**

**#35 A Very Merry Christmas**

**#36 Geronimo's Valentine**

**#37 The Race Across America**

**#38 A Fabumou School Adven**

**#39 Singing Sensation**

**#40 The Karate Mouse**

**#41 Mighty Mount Kilimanjaro**

**#42 The Peculiar Pumpkin Thief**

**#43 I'm Not Supermous**

**44 The Giant
mond Robbery**

**#45 Save the White
Whale!**

**#46 The Haunted
Castle**

**#47 Run for the Hills,
Geronimo!**

**#48 The Mystery in
Venice**

**49 The Way of
the Samurai**

**#50 This Hotel Is
Haunted!**

**#51 The Enormouse
Pearl Heist**

**#52 Mouse in Space!**

**#53 Rumble in
the Jungle**

**Get into Gear,
Stilton!**

**#55 The Golden
Statue Plot**

**#56 Flight of the
Red Bandit**

**The Hunt for the
Golden Book**

**#57 The Stinky
Cheese Vacation**

**58 The Super
hef Contest**

**#59 Welcome to
Moldy Manor**

**The Hunt for the
Curious Cheese**

**#60 The Treasure of
Easter Island**

**#61 Mouse House
Hunter**

**#62 Mouse
Overboard!**

**The Hunt for the
Secret Papyrus**

# MEET
# GERONIMO STILTONIX

He is a spacemouse — the Geronimo Stilton of a parallel universe! He is captain of the spaceship *MouseStar 1*. While flying through the cosmos, he visits distant planets and meets crazy aliens. His adventures are out of this world!

#1 Alien Escape

#2 You're Mine, Captain!

#3 Ice Planet Adventure

#4 The Galactic Goal

#5 Rescue Rebellion

#6 The Underwater Planet

#7 Beware! Space Junk!

Be sure to read all of our magical special edition adventures!

**THE KINGDOM OF FANTASY**

**THE QUEST FOR PARADISE:**
THE RETURN TO THE KINGDOM OF FANTASY

**THE AMAZING VOYAGE:**
THE THIRD ADVENTURE IN THE KINGDOM OF FANTASY

**THE DRAGON PROPHECY:**
THE FOURTH ADVENTURE IN THE KINGDOM OF FANTASY

**THE VOLCANO OF FIRE:**
THE FIFTH ADVENTURE IN THE KINGDOM OF FANTASY

**THE SEARCH FOR TREASURE:**
THE SIXTH ADVENTURE IN THE KINGDOM OF FANTASY

**THE ENCHANTED CHARMS**
THE SEVENTH ADVENTURE IN THE KINGDOM OF FANTASY

**THE PHOENIX OF DESTINY:**
AN EPIC KINGDOM OF FANTASY ADVENTURE

**THEA STILTON: THE JOURNEY TO ATLANTIS**

**THEA STILTON: THE SECRET OF THE FAIRIES**

**THEA STILTON: THE SECRET OF THE SNOW**

**THEA STILTON: THE CLOUD CASTLE**